Kelp, Ollie,
use their Unicorn Spark
to knock down acorns.

Kelp makes a bubble.

DREAMWORKS

Not Quite Narwhal

Kelp Leads the Way!

Adapted by Maggie Testa
Based on the original book by Jessie Sima

Ready-to-Read

Simon Spotlight
New York   London   Toronto   Sydney   New Delhi

SIMON SPOTLIGHT

An imprint of Simon & Schuster Children's Publishing Division

1230 Avenue of the Americas, New York, New York 10020

This Simon Spotlight edition May 2024

DreamWorks Not Quite Narwhal © 2024 DreamWorks Animation LLC.

All Rights Reserved.

All rights reserved, including the right of reproduction in whole or in part in any form.

SIMON SPOTLIGHT, READY-TO-READ, and colophon are registered trademarks of Simon & Schuster, LLC.

Simon & Schuster: Celebrating 100 Years of Publishing in 2024

For information about special discounts for bulk purchases, please contact Simon & Schuster Special Sales at 1-866-506-1949 or business@simonandschuster.com.

Manufactured in the United States of America 0324 LAK

10 9 8 7 6 5 4 3 2 1

ISBN 978-1-6659-5124-1 (hc)

ISBN 978-1-6659-5123-4 (pbk)

ISBN 978-1-6659-5125-8 (ebook)

It does not hit
any acorns.

Kelp tries again.

He makes so many
bubbles that he
loses control.

The bubbles hit
a big rock!
Oh no!

The rock blocks the waterfall that gives glimmer to Glimmer Glen.

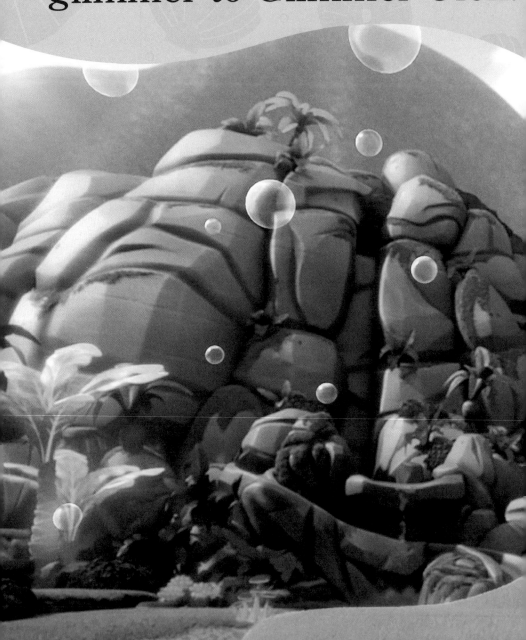

"We can move the rock
if we put our Spark
together," says Pixie.

"I do not want
to use my Spark again
today," says Kelp.

"You can move the rock without using your Spark," Cruz says.

The unicorns climb
up the cliff.
Kelp leads the way!

The unicorns push
through the bushes.

Kelp leads the way!

The rock is on
the other side
of a big jump.

How will they get across?

They can swing
on the vines!

They did it!

They try pushing
the rock.

It does not move.

"We cannot move the rock without using our Spark," says Kelp.

"We cannot quit now,"
says Ollie. Ollie jumps
off the big rock.

Ollie lands on the
dirt near the rock.
The rock moves a little.

Kelp has an idea.

The unicorns dance
in front of the rock.
The dirt moves more.

Then the rock rolls
away. The waterfall
flows again!

Kelp wants to use his Spark again! He leads the way back to Glimmer Glen.